The 1st Goopy, Goofy, Loopy Adventure

Volume 1

The 1st Goopy, Goofy, Goofy, Loopy Adventure

Volume 1

Story by Erica Orloff

Based on the characters created by Tony DiLoia

ANIMAGIC

ENTERTAINMENT GROUP, INC.

Visit our web site: www.balloonatiks.com

Cover and interior book design by Tim Kaage, LaurelGraphx, Inc.

Tony Diloia
Animagic Entertainment Group
(805) 898-1950
(805) 898-1921 (FAX)
22 W. Mission St., Suite C2
Santa Barbara, CA 93101
E-mail: diioia@aol.com

Jay Poynor
Animagic Entertainment Group
(212) 327-0998
(212) 734-5909 (FAX)
444 East 82nd St., Suite 28C
New York, NY 10028
E-mail: jpoynor@webspan.net

Dedicated to the founding members
of the Balloonatiks fan club:

Bailey, Lija, Kalia, Rowan
Alexa, Nicholas, and Isabella

Acknowledgments

We would like to thank our designer,
Tim Kaage of LaurelGraphx, Inc. Tony extends special
thank you's to Vicki, Jay Poynor, Walt, Judy and Glenn.
Erica, as always, thanks her parents and family, especially
her kids for putting up with Mom's crazy deadlines.

Table of Contents

CHAPTER 1

Afterschool Experiments

"You are NOT going to dissect this poor frog!!" Nicole Gonzales squealed at the four other students in Professor Swellhead's after-school science lab.

"Calm down, Nic," said Roosevelt Vix, Hot Air High's resident super-jock, "it's only a frog."

"But he's so cute, aren't you, fella?" Nic leaned in closer. "If I kiss him, do you think he'll turn into a prince?"

"Not likely," said Gary Zikowski, class brain, "frog DNA and human DNA are vastly different and . . ."

"Puh-leeze! Spare us the long-winded

explanations!" Roosevelt sighed. "Look, ol' R.V. here needs to finish all his labs TODAY or I can't play in the football game this Saturday. So we're dissecting this frog, and we're getting the extra credit, and I'm heading home so I can eat. Man, I'm starving."

"Please don't mention food. I'm craving a cranberry and pickle pizza," whined Randy Windbag. Randy was the son of Hot Air's mayor, and cooking strange foods was his favorite pastime.

"EWWWWW!" squealed the fifth student staying after school, none other than Sandy Readington, head cheerleader and student council president. "Come on, let's all get along," she smiled. "No bickering, please." She smiled even brighter.

Nic just rolled her eyes. She was the class actress, singer and activist. "Different" was her favorite way to dress, while Sandy only wore the most perfectly matched, designer outfits.

"Just what are you doing here anyway, Miss Perfect Pants? Don't you already HAVE straight A's?"

"Why yes I do, as a matter of fact," Sandy said sweetly. "But a person can never have too much extra credit."

"Spare me," moaned R.V. "I'll be lucky if I pass Professor Swellhead's chemistry class this semester."

With that, their teacher came zooming into class on a super hot-air powered skateboard. Professor Swellhead was like no other teacher the kids had ever met. He was a genius—a super-genius!—and every minute of every day he was working on inventions and problems and equations. But he was also a skateboard wiz, a surfer, and the best miniature golf player in Hot Air City. Rumors were whispered that he had been Hot Air's leading student activist back when he was in school. All the kids knew was that he could do a handstand while telling them about science, ride a skateboard while solving an equation that filled up an entire blackboard, and somehow make science class fun.

"Roosevelt, Gary, Sandy, Nicole, Randy," he nodded at his five favorite students. He was wearing his "lucky experiment shirt," a Hawaiian print so bright you practically needed sunglasses to look at it. "I'm so happy you came to my after-school lab today. I promise you this will be cool."

"Um . . . Professor Swellhead, sir?" Nicole raised her hand.

"Yes, Nicole?"

"Professor, I just want to say that I'm technically NOT here to dissect this frog for extra credit, or to dissect anything for that matter. You know how I feel about dissection and animal experiments."

"Yes, I am quite aware of that. I applaud your activism. Reminds me of the time I had a sit-in in the mayor's office to protest drilling the land in Hot Air's bird sanctuary."

R.V. complained, "Yeah, well, her activism can get on my nerves! Remember the time she gave a speech on animal rights and she spoke for . . . like an hour . . . the ENTIRE class time."

"I kind of liked that speech," Randy Windbag said. "I didn't have my homework done that day."

Nic glared at R.V. and said, "I'm just here to register my complaints and to officially protest this lab."

"Good for you, Nicole," Professor Swellhead said, "I admire students who express their beliefs."

Professor Swellhead was like that. He was a teacher who loved teaching more than anything else—except maybe inventing. His grandfather had been an inventor, too. In fact, his grandfather had discovered all of the natural gases and minerals beneath Hot Air City way back when. That made his grandfather a zillionaire—or something like that. And Professor Swellhead was the richest man in town. Yet he still taught his students and worked hard every day.

"Well class, I am most excited for today's experiments. In addition to the frog lab, we will be working on my top-secret latex experiment. I am inventing a rubber-like substance, and when this experiment works, we shall have a valuable and revolutionary product that will transform the way we drive cars—and maybe help clean up the environment as well!"

"No offense, Professor, but didn't you say your Super Secret High-Tech Revolutionary Wonder Gel would save the ozone?" asked Randy.

"And didn't it make the principal's hair fall out when he smelled it?" asked R.V.

"And what about the time you accidentally left the lock off the mouse experiment?" asked Sandy.

"Approximately 300 mice of abnormally high intelligence were turned loose," Gary looked up from his book long enough to remember the day. "Four teachers and eleven students fainted from the scare. A few mice are STILL loose in the school somewhere."

"Let's not forget the time you invented the vitamin potion that was supposed to help the football team win the game," R.V. pointed out.

"Yeah," said Nic. "You got it confused with your laughing potion, and they spent the whole game laughing so hard they fell down."

"We lost 112 to 3!" said R.V.

"And the self-flushing toilet . . . remember that?" asked Randy.

"EWWWWWWWWWWWWWW!" Sandy squealed. "Let's not even discuss that disaster."

Professor Swellhead laughed along with the students. "Yes, but in order to discover greatness, my friends, you must be willing to make mistakes, to experiment, to try new things. Remember when they said this city couldn't be run on thermal hot air power? It took me eighty-nine tries, but I finally figured out how to do it. That, my young friends, is science! Besides, I am sure this is going to work. Come and look."

The kids gathered around the lab table. "It looks like electric green GOOP!" said Randy.

"Goop. Interesting term. Goop! I like it. You kids go on and start the frog experiment, while I continue looking at the formula."

Randy, Sandy, R.V. and Nic gathered around the frog, while Gary stayed at Professor Swellhead's lab table.

"Professor?"

"Yes, Gary?" His teacher beamed with pride. Gary was the smartest student he had ever taught. In fact, Gary had skipped two whole grades and was still the best student in the class.

"I've been examining your formula calculations and comparing them to some of Albert Einstein's work. Everything looks like it should work. But I can't understand why your rubber mixture is so hot. Look at it. Its thermal properties are way too high. What could have gone wrong?"

Professor Swellhead looked down at the bubbling, bright green mixture. "I don't know. It does seem too hot. If I didn't know any better, I'd say someone has been tampering with this. Like that evil Dr. Poppemoff. But that's impossible. I have the only key to this room."

With that, Professor Swellhead took the key out of his packet. Then he put it back and took out a handkerchief and blew his nose. "This darn cold, Gary. I'm not thinking as clearly as I should. Let's look at the formula again. Better yet, let me ride my skateboard around the room. I think better when I'm moving." He hopped on his electric blue board and started skating around the classroom.

Meanwhile, R.V., Sandy, and Randy were arguing with Nic.

"I'm telling you, dissecting this frog is wrong!"

"So is failing science class," said Randy and R.V. in unison.

Nic didn't want to hear it. She grabbed the frog and put it on the floor. "Run, froggy, run! Be free! Save the frog!"

"Run, Nicole? Run?" asked Sandy. "Nicole, frogs hop."

"Okay frog, hop. Hop away. Be free!"

As if he understood her, the frog jumped as high and as fast as it could. R.V. and Randy chased after it, while Nicole chased THEM, still shouting, "Be free! Be free!" R.V., the forty-yard-dash champ of the football team caught the frog, just as Randy bent down to try to catch it, too. The two boys bumped heads, causing R.V. to fling the frog toward Professor Swellhead as he skated past.

"Watch out!" screamed Nic. The frog hit their teacher square in the face so he couldn't see where he was skating. "WHOA!!!!!!!!!!!" Professor screamed, waving his arms wildly to keep from crashing. Just then, Professor Swellhead felt an immense sneeze coming on.

It all happened in the blink of an eye.

The frog, in a panic, jumped from the professor and into the bubbling concoction of electric green goop . . .

. . . just as all the students reached the lab table

. . . just as Gary figured out that the formula was unstable

. . . just as Professor Swellhead let out the mother of all sneezes, crashing into the lab table, launching a nose hair into the mixture

. . . just as the frog was trying to leap out of the goop.

It was a chain reaction.

Goop flew everywhere. But most importantly, all five students were gooped at the same time . . . covered in Professor Swellhead's strange and mysterious slimy formula.

"GROSS!" squealed Sandy. But her voice sounded funny.

Something was wrong.

Something was very wrong.

The students and the frog were transforming in front of Professor Swellhead's eyes.

"So much for my 'lucky experiment shirt,'" he said in a panic. "This—most definitely—was NOT supposed to happen!"

CHAPTER 2

Gooped!!!

"Where's a mirror? I need a mirror!" Sandy shrieked. "I have . . . GOOP . . . in my hair. Oh this is gross. I can't believe it! I feel so SLIMY!!"

R.V. looked down at himself and then over at Sandy. "You got a lot more problems than your hair, Sandy."

"What? WHAT!" Her voice grew more high-pitched. "Professor Swellhead, is there a mirror in here?"

Professor Swellhead looked at his students . . . who now didn't look anything like his students. "Perhaps you should wait a minute, Sandy. You've

had a little scare. I don't want you getting even more upset."

"I can't possibly be any more upset than I am right now! I've been GOOPED! Gooped! A girl like me simply can't be seen looking like a wreck. I have a reputation to uphold. I've got to get this goop out of my hair. Right now. This instant."

"Very well . . . " the professor sighed. "But I don't think you're going to be very happy, Sandy."

"That's an understatement," R.V. muttered.

"There's a mirror inside that back closet," Professor Swellhead said.

Sandy and the others raced over to the closet and opened the door. All five of them stared at their reflections in the full-length mirror.

"Tell me this isn't happening!" shouted Nicole.

"Wh--wh--what ha--ha--happened? Wh--wh--what am I?" wondered Randy.

"Oh my gosh, I've got a serious crisis on my hands! What am I supposed to do? Nothing will color-coordinate with this disastrous outfit." Sandy squealed.

"Professor?" Asked R.V., "What's going on?"

"Well, um, ahem . . . it appears that my calculations for the latex were too unstable. Somehow, you five have been transformed into . . . rubber creatures."

"Creatures? We're creatures? My Mom's gonna freak!" said Nicole.

"Perhaps we should call you balloon people. 'Creatures sounds' . . . a little unpleasant," their teacher said.

"Unpleasant. Unpleasant! You call coming to school one day and ending up a balloon person 'unpleasant'? That's an understatement. This is a DISASTER!" Sandy squeaked. Her voice was so high-pitched the others grimaced.

"My father will be a lunatic when he finds out," said R.V.

"That's it!" said Gary.

"That's what?" asked R.V.

"We're most definitely not balloon people," he said as he pulled on his arm and watched it stretch to the ground. "We're insane balloons. Strange balloons. Weird balloons. We're Balloonatiks!"

"You *would* think it's cool," snapped R.V. "You're a twelve-year-old genius. You're a book-worm. I, myself, have a reputation to protect. I'm a football god around here, and I sure can't be catching any footballs with this arm." R.V. stretched his arm and watched it jiggle.

"Well," sniffed Sandy, "I for one am not going to stay a Balloonatik or whatever you want to call yourself Gary. I'm changing back to Sandy Readington. So go ahead Professor Swellhead.

Zap me back to Sandy. Beam me up. Whatever it is you science professors do. Change me back."

Professor Swellhead looked totally dejected.

"I'm waiting, Professor. Any minute now. Zap me."

Professor Swellhead looked down at the ground and spoke very softly.

"I am afraid I can't do that, Sandy."

"Excuuuuuuuuuse me?" asked Nicole.

"What do you mean, Professor?" Sandy chimed in, her voice decidedly squeakier than usual. "Just change us back from Balloonatiks or whatever Gary wants to call us, to our regular selves."

"It's not that simple, I'm afraid."

"Why not Professor?" asked R.V. "I'm some kind of blue rubber dude now. How am I supposed to play in Saturday's game?"

"Chain reaction."

"Chain reaction?" asked R.V., Randy, Sandy and Nicole in unison.

"What the professor is trying to tell you guys," said Gary, "is he doesn't know what happened.

A chain of events was set into motion. There was the frog . . . the temperature of the goop . . . the sneeze. And there's no way of telling precisely what happened without more experiments to duplicate what took place. According to my calculations . . ." and with that Gary reached with a long rubbery arm across the classroom to his notebook.

"Look Airbrain, I don't need any long-winded explanation. Just tell me how it is we get back to how we were," R.V. folded his rubberized arms across his chest.

"We don't know," said Gary, "at least not yet. What the professor and I are trying to tell you is we need to redo the experiment to figure out what went wrong. Speaking of which, Professor Swellhead, where's the frog?"

The five Balloonatiks looked around the room for a little green frog.

"Over there!" Sandy shrieked. The other Balloonatiks covered their ears.

"Stop shrieking! You're killing my ears. You sound like helium gone crazy!" shouted R.V. But they all spotted the frog.

"He's been gooped, too!" shouted Randy.

"Catch him!" screamed Nicole.

"And quick," shouted their teacher. "If we're ever to get you all back into human form, we need that frog!"

The five Balloonatiks and Professor Swellhead scrambled all around the chemistry lab in an attempt to catch the frog. But a rubberized frog is even more slippery than a regular frog. The green frog could now bounce from floor to ceiling. He could hop on the ceiling, stick to windows, bounce like a rubber ball. Professor Swellhead jumped on his motorized skateboard and raced around the class. Finally, he caught him, but the frog slipped out of the professor's grasp.

"Get him, R.V.!" Professor Swellhead yelled at the school's star athlete. R.V., with his excellent football and baseball catching abilities, at last caught the frog like a catcher saving a home run play.

"GOTCHA!"

Professor Swellhead took the frog from R.V. and placed him in an aquarium.

"If we're to duplicate the experiment, we better save this little frog here. Right fella?" he asked the frog. The frog seemed to understand. He nodded. The frog seemed just as confused as the students by his new shape.

"OK, back to more practical matters, Professor. Just how long will it take you and Airbrain here to duplicate the experiment. 'Cause I figure I only have about an hour or so before I have to go home for dinner," R.V. said, looking at the clock on the wall.

"DINNER!" Randy grabbed at his now enormous rubbery stomach. "Please don't mention dinner. I told you I wanted a cranberry and pickle pizza. But the way this day is going, I think I really need a triple-decker Swiss cheese, grape jelly, tuna fish sandwich—with a side of onions and a chocolate and mustard milkshake." He watched his stomach bounce up and down, shaking like a bowl of gelatin.

"I'm afraid repeating the chain reaction won't be so simple. It could take days . . . weeks . . . months," Professor Swellhead gulped. They could barely hear him as he whispered, "Years."

"YEARS!" Nicole and Sandy shrieked in unison.

"I'll miss the prom!"

"I'll miss singing with my band, The Peace Pipes, at the annual Battle of the Bands. And this year I was sure we were going to win."

With that, Nicole slapped her hands together in frustration. To her shock and everyone's horror, a lightning bolt flew from her fingertips and sizzled across the room, nearly catching Professor Swellhead's ponytail on fire.

"Whoa!" said R.V.

"It's like static electricity from a balloon—only magnified a hundred times," said Gary. "Pretty cool!"

"Yeah guys," said Professor Swellhead, "it is what you call 'cool.' But you all should be really careful until we know precisely how this transformation has effected each of you. I'll have to study you one at a time until we know exactly what you can and can't do, and," he patted his burned hair, "what we should be careful of."

"So what are we supposed to do now?" moaned Randy.

"There's nothing to do," said R.V. "We're stuck as Ballonatiks until Professor Swellhead and Airbrain here can figure out a way to UN-GOOP us. Until then, we're going to be the laughing-stocks of the whole school."

Professor Swellhead did a handstand. He always thought better when he was upside-down. "At least it's Friday. I have until Monday to figure something out. Until then, be very careful. And don't get stuck with any pins or popped or any-thing. I don't know yet how you guys work."

R.V. looked in the mirror one last time. "I'm not playing in the football game, I guess. I might as well *be* a football. They can toss me around during the game."

Dejectedly the five students turned to leave.

"I promise you," said Professor Swellhead said, walking on his hands around the room, "I will put all my considerable brain power to figuring out a solution to our problem. I will not rest until I find the answer."

"Thanks, Professor," said Randy.

"Yeah," said Gary. "We don't blame you. We know you're the best professor Hot Air High has ever seen."

The five students left the classroom. Professor Swellhead did a flip and stood back up. He turned to the frog. "Well, my little green rubber fellow, I guess it's time to do some more research."

The frog just looked at the professor and belched.

Professor Swellhead turned his back to the frog and turned his attention to the beaker that used to contain the goop experiment.

"Back to the drawing board," he sighed. "Because I can't let those kids down. I just can't. I guess we'll be ordering in pizza and staying up all night."

The frog peeked over the top of his aquarium. He spit a stream of water at the professor.

"Yes . . . Leaky," Professor Swellhead shook his head, "I suppose it does seem hopeless. But the Balloonatiks need me. Now let's try that experiment again . . . "

CHAPTER 3

Can Flator Play Football?

"Now let me get this straight, Roosevelt," R.V.'s father said, looking at his bright blue Balloonatik son. "You were accidentally turned into a balloon. And now you're stuck this way until Professor Swellhead can reverse the . . . what did you call it? Chain reaction?"

"Something like that, Dad." R.V. was now shrinking smaller and smaller. The more depressed he got over his new Balloonatik status, the more he shrank.

"Can I bring you in for Show and Tell?" his younger brother, George, giggled with delight. "I can't WAIT to tell everyone about this." He slapped his knee, laughing hysterically.

R.V. felt himself get angry. Really mad. And the madder he got, the more he grew. He inflated and inflated, filling his living room.

"You better not tell anyone about this! No one. You hear me, George?"

George just stared up at his by-now HUGE big brother, who was as tall as the ceiling and still inflating. George just nodded.

R.V.'s mother stared at her son. "Roosevelt! You just deflate right this instant! I mean it young man! Deflate. Shrink! I can't have you hogging up the living room being some supersized whoopee cushion. Now get back down to normal."

"How do I do that?"

"I don't know. You're the balloon, Roosevelt."

Roosevelt's mom tapped her foot, waiting for R.V. to shrink. He knew a tapping foot meant she was really mad!. R.V. thought about it. That's it!

Mad! Suddenly, he realized something. When he was mad, he expanded. When he was sad and feeling low, he shrank. He started thinking about not playing in Saturday's football game. He started thinking about how he was no longer R.V., cool dude on campus. He was now . . . what? An inflatable Balloonatik. Yup, things couldn't be any worse. And as R.V. thought all these thoughts, he began to shrink. Slowly he came down to normal size.

"Good," his mother said. "Now are you going to sit down and eat with us? I made your favorite: steak and potatoes! And apple pie for dessert."

"No thanks, Ma. I've had a terrible day. I'm not hungry. I'm going up to my room."

"Can I have R.V.'s steak, Ma? Can I?" asked George.

"Hush George! Can't you see your brother is upset?"

Once in his own bedroom, R.V. flopped down on his bed and stared up at the ceiling. His room was a shrine to his own athletic godliness. Football trophies lined the shelves. Baseball trophies lined the bookcases. Posters filled every available inch of wall space . . . all his favorite sports teams and sports stars. Then there was his spectacular collection of "slightly used" athletic socks worn by the greatest football players of all time. Sports was his life. Truth was, without being a football hero, R.V. didn't know who he really was or what he wanted to do. What could he be as a Balloonatik? There were no Balloonatik Olympics. No Balloonatik professional football teams. Face it, as a Balloonatik, he was all washed up. An inflatable toy. A Flator! Once everyone in Hot Air City found out about this, he'd just be Flator.

He sat up. What did he always do when he was feeling down? He lifted weights. R.V. went over to his weight bench and started lifting weights.

"What?? What's going on?" He could lift more weight than usual. He felt himself increasing in size again. He was getting bigger . . . bigger. This was going to take some getting used to.

Just then, the phone rang. It was Professor Swellhead.

"Roosevelt, I am working on some ideas. Some ideas to help us. Now I need you to tell me everything you have noticed about your new self. Everything. I'm going to write down all that I can about each of you. Then I'm going to insert all the data in my top-secret computer. Perhaps my answer will be in your special powers."

"Do you really think so?" As Flator got excited, he felt himself inflate bigger.

"I really do, Roosevelt. As a scientist I have learned one very valuable thing. You never assume anything. Sometimes the answer is right under your nose, and it was there all the time, you just didn't see it."

"OK. So what do you want to know?"

"Well, remember how Nicole created a spark with her fingertips? I think each of you has special powers that somehow relate to how each of you was as an ordinary teenager. If I was going to take a guess, R.V., I would say you are superhumanly strong."

"Kind of. It's more like superhumanly sized!"

Flator went on to describe how his size changed, and how he had figured out that when he was mad or feeling confident, he grew, but when he felt down or someone—like his obnoxious kid brother—made fun of him, he shrank.

"I am very proud of you for figuring this out, R.V."

"But it still doesn't help me. I'm not R.V. anymore. I'm this inflated thing. I even thought of a name for myself. Flator. FLATOR! That's what I am. And I'm not happy about it!"

"We'll get to the bottom of this R.V. When you went home, I looked over all my notes. I also checked all of the gauges that were part of my experiment. Someone had changed them."

"What?!? You mean someone wanted us to become Balloonatiks!"

"Not exactly. My guess is whoever did this didn't want you to become balloon people. They just wanted to destroy my work or change it somehow. If I was going to take a wild guess, I'd say it was my arch-rival Dr. Poppemoff. I haven't figured out what he was up to or why. But I will. Now tell me, what else have you noticed?"

"Well, it was kind of weird. On my way home from school, I could . . . now don't think I'm crazy or anything, Pop . . . I could fly."

"Fly?"

Yup. Fly. Like a super hero. Only it was a little windy today and I ended up blowing over the garbage dump. Man, did that stink!"

"So the wind can blow you around?"

"Uh-huh. But I figure if I have to be stuck being a Balloonatik, it ain't so bad to be able to fly. I just need to learn how to steer myself."

"Well, Roosevelt . . . Flator . . . this is all very helpful to me. I have a plan."

"You do? What is it?"

"I don't know yet."

"But you said you had a plan." Flator was now very confused.

"After all my years being a scientist, I know when my brain is cooking."

"Cooking?"

"Yes. Sort of like my latex experiment. Things in my brain are bubbling right now. I am putting in all these facts . . . kind of like a soup. And when it all comes to a boil, I'll have a plan. You, Flator, are part of my soup. Thank you. I will call you before the weekend is over."

"OK, Professor. Thanks. In the meantime, I'm going to lie low. I mean, I like flying and all that, but there's no way the team would ever let me live it down if they knew I was a Balloonatik!"

"I understand. I'll work as fast as I can."

"So long, Professor." Flator hung up the phone and sighed. He started shrinking. "First I'm a Balloonatik. Now I'm part of the professor's soup. From linebacker to Balloonatik soup. This is a day for the record books!"

CHAPTER 4

From Princess to . . . Squeeker?

Mr. and Mrs. Randolph J. Worthington Smith Reed Readington III had just sat down to a scrumptious nine-course dinner served by their butler, James, when Sandy came home to the Readington mansion.

"Hi Mom! Hi Dad!" she said, walking into the dining room. She still was not used to her high-pitched, decidedly squeaky voice. Everything she said came out in a piercing squeak. Instantly, all the elegant crystal on the dining room table shattered. Water flew everywhere from the broken goblets, and James and her parents covered their ears.

Mrs. Worthington stood, clutching her pink linen napkin, "Sandy? My Sandy? What happened to your hair, darling? Your lovely nail polish? Your designer clothes? Those cute little two-hundred-dollar shoes we picked out together? Where is my perfect little Sandy?"

"Mom, it's still me . . . but something happened at school today."

Sandy explained the day's adventure to her mother and father, and James. She explained about the goop and the frog and the experiment that didn't go quite as planned. As she talked, she got upset. After all, she was now a Balloonatik instead of the most popular girl at Hot Air High School. The more upset she became, the higher-pitched her voice grew. She was squeaking at super-sonic levels, and the huge crystal chandelier in the dining room was starting to crack.

"Sandy . . . I'm begging you," her father said, "Calm down and stop squeaking. That chandelier is an eighteenth-century antique from the ball-room of a French king."

"Is that all you can think about, Randolph?" asked Mrs. Catherine Eleanor Anna Worthington Smith Reed Readington III.

"Catherine, darling, don't worry. Sandy, just go back to your normal self so you don't upset your mother. Go on . . . up to your room and change back to a human."

"It's not that simple, Dad. Professor Swellhead is working on it."

"Working on it? Oh Sandy," her mother sobbed, "I was certain you were going to win the Miss Hot Air City contest. You remember that I won that contest when I was a young girl, and it was the start of my beauty pageant career. If you had won, we'd be the first mother-daughter winners in the history of the pageant. And now . . . now . . . you're a squeaking rubber person."

With that, Mrs. Catherine Eleanor Anna Worthington Smith Reed Readington III, who still wore her Miss Hot Air City sash around her elegant velvet dinner dress, fainted into the arms of her husband.

"I better get her upstairs so she can lie down," said Sandy's father, lifting his wife and carrying her up the huge marble staircase to the second floor of the mansion.

Sandy stood dejectedly in her family's dining room. "I guess I'll just go up to my room, James."

"Don't worry, Miss Sandy. I'll have the cook prepare you a tray of your favorite foods. You still like peppermint stick ice cream even though you're a Balloonatik, don't you?"

"Yes I do, James," Sandy said, and kissed him on the cheek. "How thoughtful of you. Thanks."

"Don't worry about your parents, Sandy. If there's one thing I have learned in the thirty years I have worked for the Readingtons . . . they'll get over it. Tomorrow is your mother's garden party with the ladies of Hot Air society. She'll be all involved with her roses and petunias. She'll calm down."

"You're the best, James," Sandy said, and ran up to her room. She never fully appreciated James until now.

Sandy's room was decorated like a colorful fairy-tale dream. A carousel horse stood in one corner, and everything in the room was in designer shades of lavender and deep purple. Sandy liked color—and designer everything. Her bed was covered with designer sheets and in her drawers were designer clothes right down to her socks— with little designer labels. An enormous canopy rose almost to the ceiling. Teddy bears decorated every inch of space, along with her Hot Air High cheerleading pom-poms, her ballet shoes, her certificates of achievement from all the clubs she belonged to. At last count, Sandy was on fourteen different school committees and was a member of eight different clubs. Whatever would Hot Air High School do without her leadership? Because she would insist her father hire a tutor. There was no way she could face the cheerleading squad with . . . rubber hair. That was simply out of the question.

James brought a tray of her favorite foods, and after thanking him, she sat down on her bed and started eating her peppermint stick ice cream. Her hot-pink princess phone rang.

"Hello?" She squeaked.

"Sandy? It's Professor Swellhead."

"Hello, Professor. Excuse the squeak. You'll just have to call me Squeeker from now on."

Professor Swellhead chuckled. Then he asked her the same questions he had asked Flator.

"It's important that I understand how each of you has changed."

"Well, for one thing," Sandy sniffed, "I am not the best-dressed girl in school anymore. I mean, it's bad enough I got changed into a Balloonatik, but couldn't you have done something about the wardrobe? Latex? And not a designer label in sight!"

"Yes, I understand, Sandy. I'd be pretty depressed if I suddenly lost my favorite Hawaiian shirts."

"Professor, those shirts are so UGLY. In my case, this is SERIOUS! A girl has to look spectacular, you know?"

"Agreed. We can look into the wardrobe later. But I was thinking more about any . . . special powers. Have you noticed anything?"

"I can stretch."

"Stretch?"

"I guess it comes from all those years doing backflips and cartwheels and splits for cheerleading. As a Balloonatik, I can stretch myself like a giant rubber band. I can stretch myself to the sky. But it's not like the cheerleading coach is going to be happy about that."

"No. I guess not."

"And my voice breaks crystal."

"Breaks crystal, you say?"

"Yes. It broke all my mother's crystal today. And I'm pretty sure there's no way my father's going to let me in the dining room again. He has an expensive chandelier in there. All crystal."

"That would be a problem. I remember riding my first skateboard over a ramp I set up and right into my mother's favorite lily garden."

"Exactly. My parents aren't exactly too. I also noticed that when I am upset and my voice gets

very squeaky . . . traffic lights stop working.
Electrical things seem to get . . . confused around
me. I tried to turn on the TV in my room, but
when I said something to James, the TV shorted
out. I don't even want to try to turn on my computer."

"Very interesting," Professor Swellhead said.

"I also was trying to keep calm on my way
home from school. So I started singing a little
song. A cheer, actually, from the cheerleading
squad. Well, with each squeak, DOGS started fol-
lowing me. You know . . . like a dog whistle."

"Now THAT'S pretty amazing," Professor
Swellhead said, furiously taking notes in his notebook.

"It was embarassing. I have a reputation to
uphold. And these weren't pedigreed poodles like
my Fifi. She's a little white, adorable ball of fluff.
No . . . these were any old dogs. Of uncertain
pedigree. They're all out on our lawn right now.
Do you know how that must look to the neighbors?"

"I'm certain the neighbors haven't noticed."

"The dogs are howling, Professor. This Squeeker thing is not very elegant. I mean, I plan to be a professional manners consultant when I grow up. Not a dog catcher."

"Perhaps there's some way we can use your squeakiness to do some good."

"How?"

"I haven't quite figured that out yet. But I will."

"Professor?"

"Yes, Squeeker?"

Squeeker sighed, "Do you think you'll be able to get us back to normal? Soon?"

"I hope so. I'll certainly do my best."

"Do you still have on your lucky experiment shirt?"

"Yes, I do," he said proudly.

"Well, maybe you should take it off. You know this whole Balloonatiks thing wasn't all that lucky."

"I hear you. Time for a new shirt. Thanks Squeeker."

Squeeker hung up the phone and looked

around her room. "Why? Why me?"

She flopped backwards on her bed. "I mean, if I had to be a Balloonatik, why couldn't I be hot pink or aqua or some really cool color? Now I even clash with my own room. How can I be perfect when I'm this ghastly yellow and orange? How can I be perfect?"

With that, her voice caused the electricity in the Readington mansion to short out. Squeeker sat in the dark.

"First I get goop in my hair . . . now I'm a Balloonatik sitting in the dark. Could things be any worse?" she wailed.

Next, all the dogs on the Readington lawn began to howl. And from down the hall, she heard her mother ordering James to chase the dogs away. Squeeker looked out the window. James and the cook were trying to chase the dogs off the Readington estate. The dogs refused to budge. Squeeker started laughing. One of her laughing-squeaks turned all the power back on again.

Squeeker laughed again, "This is the most commotion the Readington mansion has seen since a circus troupe performed for the guests at great-grandfather's wedding and a Bengal tiger got loose."

She sat back down on her perfect designer bed. "Maybe this will do us Readingtons some good."

Squeeker laughed to herself again. "If only great-grandfather could see me now!"

CHAPTER 5

A Blown-up Brain

Gary Zikowski's father was helping his nine-year-old sister, Wendy, do her calculus homework when Gary came home. Wendy was a genius, too. Gary's dad heard the door slam, but he didn't look up from the math problem.

"Gary . . . good . . . you're home. Wendy has a killer calculus problem. What do you think of using x to solve for y in a case where the numerator—"

Wendy had looked up. Her mouth hung open as she stared at her Balloonatik brother. She tapped her father on the arm.

"Wendy . . . stop it. Pay attention to the problem. OK, now if x and y are equal . . . Wendy, what's gotten into you?"

Finally Mr. Zikowski looked up.

"Gary! What happened to you?" His father's eyes widened, and he accidentally knocked his own glasses off his nose.

"Chemistry mishap." Gary shrugged.

"You're . . . you're . . ." Wendy pointed at her brother.

"A Balloonatik. Rubberized . . . full of air. R.V. called me an Airbrain."

Mr. Zikowski put his head in his hands. He had high hopes that Gary would finish high school before he was fourteen and then attend a college and become a scientist.

"Gary . . . this will not look good on your college applications."

"I kind of like it, Dad. Look at this!" Gary held his breath and started lifting off the ground.

"Neat trick," Wendy grinned. "What else can you do?"

"What else can he do! What else can he do!" Mr. Zikowski spluttered. "Wendy, your brother is not a . . . a . . .toy! He's not a dog that can do tricks! He's a boy genius. And you and he are going to go on to do great things."

"I still can do all those things, Dad. I just can also do this . . ." with that Gary exhaled and blew Wendy across the room. She giggled and clapped her hands.

"Do it again, Gary!" she squealed. "Do it again!"

"He will do nothing of the sort. Gary, you march up to your room right now and write me a 500-word essay on why it is not a good thing to be made of rubber!"

"Oh Dad . . . you're no fun!" Gary moped. He took his backpack full of schoolbooks and headed upstairs. His father meant well. Gary knew that. His father was a genius, too. Books and studying were his life. He assumed that books and studying were all Wendy and Gary cared about, too. And the truth was, Gary did love books.

But he loved Sandy Readington more. Not that she ever gave him the time of day. Actually, Gary thought, that wasn't true. Whenever she needed extra tutoring in science, she always called on Gary to help her pull through.

Gary's room looked like a laboratory. On the windowsill, he was growing bean plants that he had fed with a new plant food he had invented. The bean plants were growing so large, in fact, that they were taking over that corner of his room.

On his desk, he had a variety of experiments, all growing in containers and bottles of all shapes and sizes. On the wall hung dozens of blue ribbons he had won at science fairs. Since Gary was seven years old, no one else had ever won Hot Air City's Annual Science Contest.

On another wall hung all of Gary's certificates of achievement. He always made straight A's. Gary had three pictures in frames that he kept on his night-stand. One was of his mother. She and Gary's father were divorced and, as she was a scientist too, she was off on a mission in the jun-

gles to find rare plants. He was staying with his dad until she returned. Another picture was of Professor Swellhead and Gary standing in front of their life-size replica of a dinosaur that they had built. Gary admired Professor Swellhead more than anyone. He was the smartest man Gary had ever met. Considering both his parents were geniuses that meant he was pretty darn smart!

The third picture was kind of a secret. It was a picture of Sandy that he cut out of the school yearbook. Every time Gary looked at that picture, he sighed.

The phone rang, and Gary's computer automatically answered it and spoke in an electronic computer voice: "You have reached the private phone line of Gary Zikowski. State your name, please."

"This is Professor Swellhead. Is Gary home?"

Gary spoke to his computer, "I'll take the call."

"Gary?"

"Yes, Professor?"

"Hello. The reason I am calling is that you, of all the kids, will understand how important it is—"

"—to figure out how we have been transformed." Gary finished the professor's sentence, because he had already thought of that.

"Excellent, Gary. What have you observed?"

"For one thing, if I hold my breath, I can float. Like a blimp."

"A blimp? How curious."

"I also have to watch it. If I inhale too deeply my head expands."

"Must be all those brains, Gary."

"Precisely, Professor. That's why R.V. called me Airbrain."

"Airbrain . . . cool nickname given the circumstances. OK. What else have you noticed?"

"When I exhale, I can blow my sister clean across the room. I tried it outside, and I made two cats and a dog fly. It was an accident. They're OK."

"Good. We wouldn't want Hot Air Animal Control to be upset with us!"

"That's not all. When I inhaled, I swallowed a bicycle. And when I looked down, my body was shaped like a bicycle."

"What did you do?"

"I spit it out, of course."

"Airbrain, I'm going to need all your help unraveling the chain reaction."

"Sure, Professor. But I have to tell you . . . I like being a Balloonatik. Face it, I'm a twelve-year-old kid in high school. No one pays any attention to me, unless they want a tutor. I'm small, and I get squashed between all the football players in the hallways. But as a Balloonatik . . . well, all of a sudden I'm special."

"You are already special Gary. You have a brilliant mind."

"I know that. But you have to admit, to be able to float and do all those other things . . . well, I feel on top of the world. I'm coooooooool!"

"Cool," the professor sighed. "Yes, I know how important cool is. You'll still help me won't you?"

"Oh sure, Professor. I already made some calculations about the heat factor during the experiment."

"Excellent. I knew I could count on you, Airbrain."

"No problem!"

Gary and Professor Swellhead said good-bye. Then Gary sat down on his bed and looked at Sandy's picture.

"We're both Balloonatiks now, Sandy," he whispered. "So maybe . . . just maybe . . . you won't think of me as a little brainy kid. Maybe you'll see we are meant to be together."

Airbrain smiled at the idea. Then he remembered something.

"Computer?"

"Yes, Gary?"

"First off, call me Airbrain from now on."

"Yes, Airbrain."

"Write me an essay. Five hundred words. On why I don't want to be made of rubber."

"Yes, Airbrain."

With that command, words began appearing on the screen. The printer turned on. Ten minutes later, Airbrain's essay was done. He took it out of the printer tray.

"Excellent, Computer. I don't mean a word of it . . . but that's OK. It'll make my dad happy."

CHAPTER 6

Sparks are Flying!

Nicole Gonzales's mother was at work at the hospital when Nic arrived home from school. She had left a note on the table:

NICOLE: CASSEROLE'S IN THE FRIDGE. HEAT ON 350 DEGREES FOR FORTY MINUTES. I SHOULD BE HOME FOR DINNER. LOVE YOU, MOM.

Nic rolled her eyes and cringed. Her mother may have been the world's greatest head nurse, but she most definitely ranked up there as one of the world's worst cooks. Opening the refrigerator, Nic peered at the casserole. It had two major

problems. One, it stank. Two, she could not identify what kind of casserole it was. No clue.

"This is not a good thing," Nicole muttered to herself. "I can't even recognize it. It's worse than the mystery meat at school!"

She pulled the casserole out and stuck a fork into it. Problem number three: It was as watery as soup.

"UGH!" Nicole turned up her nose and put the casserole in the oven. Luckily for her, she kept a stash of bread and peanut butter in her room. After dinner each night she munched on peanut butter sandwiches in the privacy of her bedroom. She was proud of her Mom and would never hurt her feelings, but a girl had to eat!

Nicole shuffled her way into the living room. As she walked, like a balloon gathering static electricity, sparks flew from her feet. They flew about the room as her feet dragged along the carpet. The sparks alarmed her four cats. The cats hissed and meowed and ran around the living room looking for a hiding place. As they did so,

one knocked over a lamp and broke it into pieces, another knocked a huge pot filled with dirt to the floor (it used to contain flowers but her mother was also lousy at growing things). The third cat ran through the dirt and then through the basket of clean laundry, and the fourth cat leaped onto Nicole's mom's head JUST at the moment she was walking through the front door.

Nicole's mom screamed. Sparks were flying, a cat was on her head, her living room was a disaster area . . . and her daughter was a Balloonatik!

"Nicole Anna Maria Gonzales! What is the meaning of this?!?"

Nicole tried not to laugh at the sight of her fat orange and white tabby cat perched on her mother's head. She shrugged. "Just call me Sparky?"

Eventually, Mrs. Gonzales calmed down, and Sparky told her the whole story over dinner and then during clean-up time. Ever since her father died when she was a little girl, she and her mom were extra close. They talked about everything.

"Nicole . . . are you sure this isn't a cry for help?

Are you trying to get my attention by turning into a Balloonatik? Is that it? Am I spending too much time at the hospital?"

Sparky looked at her mother. Mrs. Gonzales was always worried that her daughter wasn't getting enough time and attention, but in truth, Mrs. Gonzales had always been there for Nicole.

"Mom, you're the best mother in the whole wide world. Just because I have to toss a casserole in the oven every now and then doesn't mean you're a bad mom. You're terrific!"

She stood up and walked over to where her mother was washing dishes after the soupy casserole and kissed her.

"Ouch!"

"What?"

"Nothing Honey. It's just you give off a little charge when you kiss me. I *am* going to have to call you Sparky from now on."

Sparky went up to her room after dinner. She was starving! As soon as she shut her door, she took out her stash of peanut butter and bread and made TWO sandwiches.

She looked around her room. Every inch of wall space contained a poster of an endangered species. From manatees to wolves, if they needed help, Sparky was writing letters to everyone from corporation presidents to the mayor of Hot Air City! She was also a poet and painter . . . and she sure could sing! She always won the lead role in the class play. Sparky looked at a photo on her desk of her singing at a local coffeehouse.

"I guess those days are over," she whispered sadly. "Who's going to come see a Balloonatik perform?"

Sparky's phone rang, and she picked it up on the first ring.

"Sparky here!"

"Sparky? I . . . uh . . . is this Nicole Gonzales?"

"Sort of."

"This is Professor Swellhead."

"Professor! Hey . . . how are you?" Sparky loved Professor Swellhead. He was also concerned about the environment and pollution. Except for the dissecting frog thing, where they never saw eye to eye, Professor and Sparky talked all the time about science and endangered species. He even gave generously when she asked for donations to Save the Sea Cow.

"I'm fine, Nicole . . . um, Sparky."

Professor Sweelhead then told her how he was gathering data on all the Balloonatiks.

"Well . . . I can tell you that walking across a carpet is downright dangerous for me. I attract static electricity like a . . . well, like a balloon. You know, where you rub them and stick them on your head. Only I send off SPARKS! And not just little sparks, Professor."

"Tell me more, Nicole," Professor Swellhead said, furiously scribbling in his notebook.

"I can even make flames! If I rub my hands together, I can create smoke . . . then sparks . . . then fire. I'm telling you, I am a Class-A explosive waiting to happen!"

"Anything else?"

Well, the neatest thing is I can make these sparks kind of turn into lightening bolts. And then . . . watch out! I'm positively electric, Professor."

"Anyone who has ever heard you sing would say that."

Sparky blushed. "Thanks, Professor. Oh . . . and one more thing. My Mom and I noticed at dishwashing time that water and Sparky don't mix to well. My sparks all went away and I got . . . I don't know, out of sorts."

"I see. Sparky, thank you. I know this all seems like a terrible mishap. It *is* a terrible mishap . . . but I'll get you all back to normal as soon as possible."

"I know you will. And listen . . . don't forget about that Save the Rainforest rally I'm organizing."

"Don't worry. I won't forget. Good night, Sparky."

"Good night, Professor."

Later that evening Mrs. Gonzales came in to kiss Sparky good night.

"Why is it I always smell peanut butter in here?"

"Mom, you always say that. I have no idea. I don't smell anything."

"Anyway, Nicole . . . Sparky, honey . . . I just want you to know that whether you're a

Balloonatik or a poet or a singer or runnin' for president someday, I'm proud of you. You're your own person. Unique and individual."

"Thanks, Mom."

"I have just one thing to ask you, Sweetie."

"Anything, Mom. Name it."

"Do me a favor and keep away from the cats for a little while."

With that Sparky and her mother threw their heads back and laughed.

CHAPTER 7

Follow the Bouncing Balloonatik: Bouncer

Randy Windbag entered the mayor's mansion. His father, the mayor of Hot Air City, was in his office, as usual, talking to three of his aides. Four telephones were ringing at once, the mayor was chewing on a cigar, and every so often, he looked up at the TV and yelled at the newsman.

"What d' ya mean I'm not going to win the election? What do you newsmen know? Of course Hot Air City will re-elect me, Mayor Windbag, the best mayor it's ever had."

Even one of his assistants rolled his eyes. The mayor had a bad habit of ignoring some of Hot Air City's most serious problems of crime, pollution, and the lack of a really good pizza parlor.

"Hey Dad," said Randy in a quiet voice. "Have a minute?"

Without even looking up, the mayor shouted, "Son, I love ya, but I don't even have a minute to talk. Have to take this call, son. A mayor's got to do what a mayor's got to do. Have to take this call . . . Mayor Windbag here . . . " he said as he picked up one of the many telephones lighting up on his desk.

Randy walked away dejected. He mimicked his father, "Son . . . I'm just super important. I know everything. I am a great man. I am a . . . sorry, there's my beeper now. A mayor's got to do what a mayor's got to do."

Sure, he knew his dad loved him. But he was always so busy. He wore a beeper in the bathroom. He even had a waterproof beeper for the shower. He never had the time to do any father-son things with Randy. He didn't even notice Randy's decidedly bouncy new Balloonatik shape.

Randy climbed up the steps to the second floor of the mansion. His mother was in her dressing room deciding on which gown to wear to the dinner she and the Mayor would be attending that night.

"Hi, Mom," Randy said.

Mrs. Windbag turned around. "RANDY! Oh dear . . . oh my . . . what on earth happened to you? Is it Halloween already?"

"No, Mom. There was kind of a little accident in science class today."

"Oh my poor baby. Let's go downstairs to the kitchen. The cook will make you a nice snack, and you can tell me all about it."

Over a snack of pizza with hot fudge and pickles on top, Randy told his mother about Professor Swellhead's experiment.

"Professor Swellhead is a brilliant man, Randy.

I'm sure he'll figure out a way to solve this. In the meantime, what will your father say? It won't look very good in an election year for the mayor to have an orange . . . rubber son. I don't know how he'll take this."

"He didn't even notice, Mom. I went into his office, and he was so busy . . . he just didn't notice. But you know his motto . . . A mayor's got to do what a mayor's got to do." As he imitated his father, he pretended to be chewing on an imaginary cigar.

Mrs. Windbag just sighed. "I'm sorry Randy. He means well. That makes me a little sad. You know, I'm going to ring for the cook and have a whatever it is you just ate, too. It's been that kind of day."

Mrs. Windbag usually hated Randy's strange food concoctions. He wanted to be a chef when he grew up, and he was always experimenting with weird recipes. But today was a pizza with hot fudge and pickles kind of afternoon. They washed down their pizza with root beer. After they had finished their pizzas, Mrs. Windbag said, "As usual, pretty weird food, Randy. But I guess today it hit the spot. I better go get ready. Are you sure you've had enough to eat?"

Randy felt his rubberized, stretchy, bouncy Balloonatik belly. "Sure have, Mom. Can't you tell? Anyway, I'm going to go upstairs to my room."

Randy's room was a top-secret place. He never let anyone in, except for his mother. Not even the maid. His room was full of whoopee cushions, chattering false teeth, and other gags. That was the joker in Randy. But the room also housed his pet hermit crabs, Seymour and Sally, and his beloved hamster, Colonel Fuzzy. He had constructed an immense hamster maze for Colonel Fuzzy that loop-de-looped and ran up to the ceiling and across the room several times and back again. He spoiled his hamster with treats. His mother wasn't too thrilled he had a "rodent" in the house, but she knew Colonel Fuzzy was a good companion for her son.

Randy reached into the hamster's favorite hiding spot and pulled his chubby hamster out.

"You're no rodent, are you Fuzzy? You're a Hamster Hero in disguise."

Randy's phone rang. Even though he had his own phone line, it rarely rang.

"Hello?" he asked, curious, as he put Colonel Fuzzy into his maze.

"Randy? It's Professor Swellhead."

"Hey Professor. You know, I'm kind of getting used to my new Balloonatik body. I think it's kind of cool."

"Tell me about it, Randy. I'm taking notes on all of you."

Randy told Professor Swellhead that he had discovered his body could function kind of like a clown's "twistee" balloon. He could make himself flatten, expand, become an oval, bounce like a ball, morph into dozens and dozens of shapes.

"Best of all, Professor, I can be a whoopee cushion. Listen . . ." Randy held the phone up to his stomach, and he made the loudest, most gurgling, ridiculous whoopee cushion sound the world has ever heard.

"PFFFFFFFFFFFFFFFFFTTTTTTTTT!!!!"

"A dubious distinction, Randy."

"What does dubious mean?"

"Rather questionable. But I can imagine the other Balloonatiks will think that's very funny."

"I'm tellin' you Professor, no more shy Randy for me. I can be the life of the party as my bouncy self."

"Yes, I'm sure you will be, Randy."

"Hey . . . I just thought of something. Don't call me Randy Windbag anymore. Just call me Bouncer."

"Bouncer it is. I can add you to Flator, Squeeker, Airbrain, Sparky and Leaky."

"Huh? Who are they?"

"The other Balloonatiks. I better get going, Bouncer. I have a long night of experimenting ahead of me. I need to find a way to change you all back. In the meantime, have fun. If you have to be a Balloonatik, you might as well enjoy it for a little while."

"No sweat, Professor."

Bouncer hung up the phone and laid down on his bed. He patted his stomach, full of pizza and pickles, and watched it jiggle around. Then he watched Colonel Fuzzy make his way through the maze. He talked to Colonel Fuzzy.

"A mayor's got to do what a mayor's got to do. That's what my father always says, Fuzzy. But you know what?" he said as he twisted his body into a pretzel shape and then made the whoopee cushion sound again. "A Bouncer's got to do what a Bouncer's got to do."

"PFFFFFFFFFFFFTTTTTTTTTTTTTTTTTTTTT!!"

Pop Swellhead's Top-Secret Notebook

Keep Out!

Flator

★ a.k.a. Roosevelt Vix

★ Flator can increase and decrease his size depending on whether he feels happy, sad, or angry.

★ He is very strong.

★ Flator is upset that he cannot play football anymore. He was a big man on campus at Hot Air High School.

★ Don't insult him—he deflates to the size of a wind-up toy.

Squeeker

- ★ a.k.a. Sandy Readington
- ★ Sandy was the most popular girl in school. She hates being a Balloonatik!
- ★ Sandy's power is her voice. She can emit a high-pitched screech that causes dogs to whimper and grown men to cover their ears, powerless. Stretching ability is incredible. She can stretch her arm across a room—or longer!
- ★ Heat and Squeeker don't mix. Heat affects her Balloonatiks powers.

Airbrain

★ a.k.a. Gary Zikowski
★ Gary is only 12 years old. He is a genius. Quite possibly the smartest student I've ever had.
★ Airbrain can hold his breath and lift himself off the ground. He can fly.
★ When Airbrain inhales, he can suck in whole objects and take their shape.
★ When Airbrain exhales, he can blow hurricane-force winds.

s

n to

make

quite a

any

at, pret-

wistee"

his name:

shakes

ait:

a giant

eard this

ate.

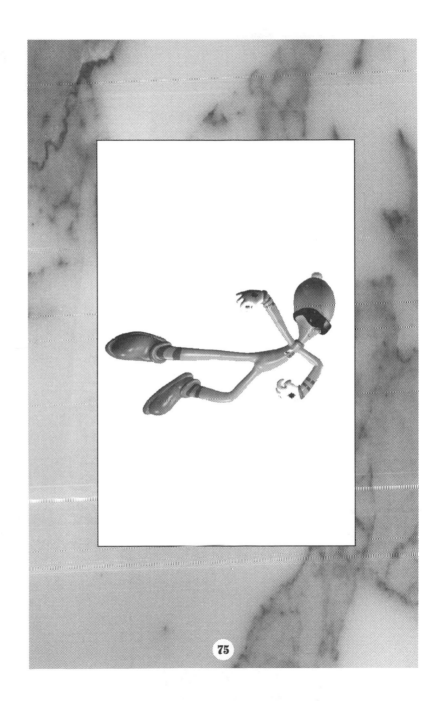

Sparky

★ a.k.a. Nicole Gonzales
★ Nicole was the class activis
and she supports many en
mental causes. She is also
poet and singer.
★ Sparky . . . her name says
She can send sparks shoo
off her feet and fingertips
can direct lightning bolts.
★ She can generate heat an
smoke by rubbing her han
together.
★ WARNING: Sparky and w
NOT mix.

Bouncer

★ a.k.a. Randy Windbag
★ Ahhh, Randy. Poor Randy. Hi
father doesn't pay attentio
him, and some of the kids
fun of his weight.
★ I have noticed Randy has
sense of humor.
★ Bouncer can morph into
shape he wants. Oval, fla
zel . . . he is a clown's "t
balloon. He is also like
bouncy. He jiggles and
like a bowl of gelatin.
★ Most embarassing tr
Bouncer can act like
whoopee cushion. I h
myself. Most indeli

Leaky

★ a.k.a. plain old frog
★ Destined to be dissected, Leaky was gooped instead and now he is a hopping, sticky, RUDE little Balloonatik.
★ He can stick to the ceiling, project himself across the room.
★ He spits.
★ He burps.
★ He insults anyone and anything in his path.
★ He is obnoxious.

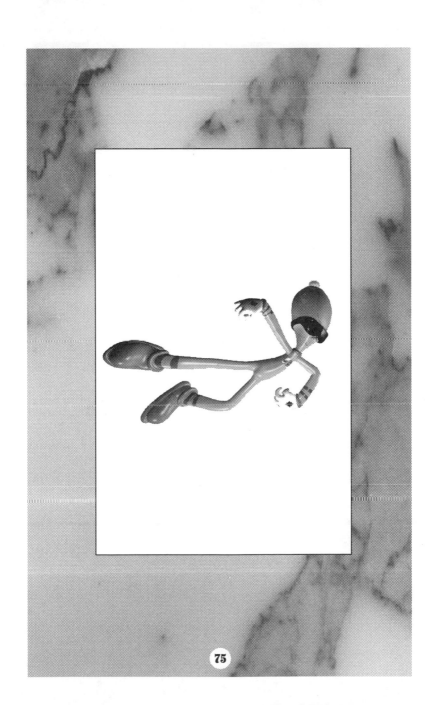

Sparky

★ a.k.a. Nicole Gonzales
★ Nicole was the class activist, and she supports many environmental causes. She is also a poet and singer.
★ Sparky . . . her name says it all. She can send sparks shooting off her feet and fingertips. She can direct lightning bolts.
★ She can generate heat and smoke by rubbing her hands together.
★ WARNING: Sparky and water do NOT mix.

Bouncer

★ a.k.a. Randy Windbag

★ Ahhh, Randy. Poor Randy. His father doesn't pay attention to him, and some of the kids make fun of his weight.

★ I have noticed Randy has quite a sense of humor.

★ Bouncer can morph into any shape he wants. Oval, flat, pretzel . . . he is a clown's "twistee" balloon. He is also like his name: bouncy. He jiggles and shakes like a bowl of gelatin.

★ Most embarassing trait: Bouncer can act like a giant whoopee cushion. I heard this myself. Most indelicate.

Leaky

★ a.k.a. plain old frog

★ Destined to be dissected, Leaky was gooped instead and now he is a hopping, sticky, RUDE little Balloonatik.

★ He can stick to the ceiling, project himself across the room.

★ He spits.

★ He burps.

★ He insults anyone and anything in his path.

★ He is obnoxious.

CHAPTER 8

Hop-A-Long Hijinks

Professor Swellhead decided he better take extra-good care of Leaky, his spitting, burping, totally rude frog. If anything happened to Leaky, Professor would not be able to re-do the experiment exactly as it had occurred. The chain reaction would be broken. The kids would be stuck forever as Balloonatiks.

On Saturday, he returned to his school laboratory and brought Leaky a special supply of plump flies. But Leaky had other ideas. He hopped over to the pizza the professor had brought for himself.

"Pizza?" asked Professor. "That's highly irregular food for a frog."

Leaky burped. Then he spit. Then he stuck his tongue out.

"In the words of Dr. Frankenstein . . . I have created a monster," sighed Professor, wearing an entirely new "lucky experiment shirt."

"Very well, Leaky. But I'll get you your own pizza, and we'll put flies on it. This one is mine and has pepperoni. So slimy frog hands off!"

As Professor turned to go, Leaky spat again.

Professor Swellhead left the room, locking the door behind him. Leaky climbed out of his aquarium tank and hopped around.

This is great, Leaky thought to himself. *I can move. I can hop on the ceiling if I want to. There is no way I'm lettin' that goofy-looking scientist turn me back into an ordinary frog. This is the life!*

Just then, someone outside in the hallway fiddled with the lock. The door opened a crack and the lights in the classroom turned off.

Leaky hopped over towards the light switch. He burped.

Then, out of the blue, someone—or something—grabbed Leaky and shoved him in a sack.

Leaky belched and even let out a croak-like scream.

Whoever took Leaky shook the sack. "Quiet in there you decidedly ridiculous little slimy frog. I've got great and evil plans for you." With that, the frog-napper and Leaky disappeared down the hall and out of Hot Air High School.

Thirty minutes later, Professor Swellhead returned with a large cheese pizza, which he smothered in flies. It smelled delicious but looked disgusting.

Professor Swellhead noticed the door was no longer locked. "Leaky? Leaky? I'm back with your pizza."

Professor Swellhead raised his eyebrows. Where was that pesky Leaky? He looked up on the ceiling and under desks. He looked in the closet and looked in his desk drawers. He was beginning to think Leaky had somehow run away. But that was impossible. This was most curious.

Then Professor Swellhead realized he'd been looking for Leaky in a half-dark classroom. He went over to the light switch and turned on the classroom lights. When he touched the switch, he felt something . . . goopy.

"What's this?" Professor Swellhead looked closer at the light switch. Yes . . . there was a drop of goop on the switch. But how was that possible?

Professor Swellhead sat down at his desk. This had been a week of disasters. First he gooped his five favorite students. Then he'd somehow lost one of the most important parts of the experiment—Leaky was gone.

Pop's head hurt.

"Maybe a slice of pizza would help," he said to himself and picked up a slice. As he bit into it, a piping hot piece of pepperoni hit the roof of his mouth. That was precisely the jolt Professor Swellhead's brain needed.

"I didn't lose Leaky! He was frog-napped! I locked the door . . . but I left the lights on. That frog was taken from here . . . by someone with an interest in my rubber experiment. Someone who knows about the goop! Someone who *has* some goop!"

Professor Swellhead had half-solved the puzzle. He knew someone had taken Leaky, but he didn't know whom. And even though he felt better that he hadn't lost Leaky, he still was minus one important piece of the puzzle. He'd have to get Leaky back. But he had no idea how. And that still left five Balloonatiks stuck that way. What would he tell Flator, Squeeker, Airbrain, Sparky, and Bouncer?

Professor Swellhead's head hurt even more. "This calls for another slice of pepperoni pizza," he said forlornly. "Those poor Balloonatiks . . ."

CHAPTER 9

Eureka!

The Swellhead Estate was located in the center of Hot Air City. Tourists always drove up to the big wrought-iron gates and peered in, because the estate was so unusual. Professor Swellhead had a full miniature golf course, including a giant spinning windmill you could see from almost anywhere in town. He had an immense skate boarding area with a giant ramp, and a wave pool so he could practice his latest surfboarding skills. He also had a pool shaped like a microscope, and a full laboratory that ran entirely on hot air power and didn't pollute the environment. But the most unusual things about the Swellhead Estate were all of Professor Swellhead's inventions. Peering through the gate, people could see robots mowing the lawn, or mechanical monkeys hanging from the trees. Inside, it was even more strange. Small trains ran around through the house carrying experiments and snacks for the professor so he didn't ever have to interrupt his work. Computers answered the phone and turned lights off and on. He even had an electric slipper warmer that warmed up his slippers like two pieces of toast in a toaster. When they popped up, they landed precisely on his feet. Professor liked inventions.

After Leaky was frog-napped, Professor Swellhead returned to his estate, very dejected. He puttered in the laboratory, but then gave up and decided to go to bed. A robot turned down his sheets and then tucked him in.

"Good night, Professor," the robot said.

"Good night XTR1000."

Professor Swellhead fell asleep but tossed and turned all night, until finally he awoke and yelled,

"Eureka!" Professor Swellhead always yelled
"Eureka!" when he thought of a really great idea.
He rushed down to his laboratory and worked for
two days straight. (When Professor Swellhead was
excited about something, he didn't sleep and he
barely ate. He also did handstands!) Finally, he
was satisfied with what he had done, and he
called each of the Balloonatiks and asked them to
meet him at his estate.

Flator, Squeeker, Airbrain, Sparky and Bouncer
waited in the professor's study.

"Why do you think he asked us here? And
you know, I'm hungry. Do you think he'll be serv-
ing snacks?" asked Bouncer.

"Use your brain, not your stomach!" snapped
Flator. "What? You think he asked us here for
dinner and a movie? He must have figured out
the formula. We're here to be turned back to the
way we were."

"You really think so?" Squeeker asked excitedly.

"Actually," Airbrain spoke, "I would think it
highly unlikely. The process of calculating the

formula is a precise and time-consuming one, and—"

"Spare me!" Sparky shouted and zapped Airbrain with a tiny spark from her fingertips.

"OUCH! What's wrong?" Airbrain asked.

"You. It's not right that some twelve-year-old kid should have so much brains."

"Stop picking on him," squeaked Squeeker, causing all the Balloonatiks to cover their ears, but Airbrain to sigh. She had defended him!

Suddenly, all five Balloonatiks were fighting and arguing. Sparky threw sparks at everyone, and Flator was growing larger by the second! Professor Swellhead walked in to the sea of commotion.

"Hey, you maniacs! What's going on?" he demanded, with a twinkle in his eye.

The five Balloonatiks stopped what they were doing (which included Bouncer SITTING on Airbrain) and stared at him.

"Nothing" they all said in unison, trying to act innocent.

"We're ready to be turned back into humans," Flator said, shrinking down to normal size.

Professor's shoulders sagged. "I'm afraid that's not going to happen. Today, at least. You see, Leaky has been frog-napped."

"Who's Leaky?" asked Sparky.

"It's the name I gave the frog. He was stolen from the classroom. By someone who has a supply of goop."

"Did you call the police?" shrieked Squeeker in alarm.

"No. The police are too busy fighting crime in Hot Air City to worry about a missing frog and some green goop."

"But without the frog, there can be no chain reaction," Airbrain said, secretly a little pleased by the news.

"That's true, Airbrain. But that's when I started thinking."

"Watch out! 'Cause when the professor thinks that's a whole lotta brain power!" said Flator. "OK, Professor. So now what?"

"After I interviewed all of you and put my findings in this notebook, I began to realize you each had a gift. Like you, Flator, you can make yourself as tall as the tallest building if you wanted. And Bouncer, you can change shape. And Sparky . . . you could make lightening bolts fly across the sky."

"Yeah, but I can't play the lead in the class play looking like this, so what good does that do me?"

"It's not what it does for you, but what you can do for others."

"HUH?!?" They all said at once.

"Just now, you were all fighting. Before you became Balloonatiks, you were all very different people. None of you, as you kids say . . . what is the word I am looking for?" Professor jumped up and flipped over and did a handstand. "Yes . . . yes . . . none of you 'hung out' with each other. But now, in one way, you're all the same: You're all Balloonatiks."

"Like I'm ever going to be the same as Bouncer here," muttered Flator. "He's a bowl of gelatin, and I'm a muscleman—a rubber one, but still a muscleman."

"I'll squash you, Flator," Bouncer said and jumped on top of him.

"Boys!" Pop Swellhead shouted. "This fighting has got to stop. You need to listen to what I am about to say."

Flator and Bouncer stopped their fighting and sat down.

"Thank you," said Pop as he continued. "Crime and pollution and problems have plagued Hot Air City since before you all were born. No offense, Bouncer, but the mayor seems to ignore some of the most important problems. But what if you, as Balloonatiks, could come together to stop these problems . . . to fight them . . . each with your own unique powers? What if you could actually do something to help others? To make the world a better place."

Sparky was the first to speak, "Helping endangered species is what I have been trying to do since I was in first grade. Maybe what you're saying isn't all that different."

"Hang ten!" said Professor Swellhead, hopping

onto a skateboard. "But before you agree, I have something else to show you. Follow me."

Professor Swellhead led the five Balloonatiks through the mansion to the west wing. He had a brand-new sign engraved over the door: "HOME OF THE BALLOONATIKS."

Once inside, five rooms opened off the hall, each with an engraved sign that read "Flator," "Squeeker," "Airbrain," "Sparky" and "Bouncer." Then, down at the end of the hall stood an enormous room. As they followed their favorite teacher inside, the Balloonatiks were shocked to see an entire wall filled with gadgets and computers and giant television monitors. Then, on the other side of the room, it was a teen's dream: ping pong tables, a pool table, a pizza oven and ice cream soda maker, comfy couches, and more video games than any of them had ever seen in their lives.

"What's this?" Squeeker asked.

"It's the new home of the Balloonatiks, I hope."

"A pizza oven . . ." Bouncer walked toward the oven as if hypnotized.

Pop laughed, "Yes . . . yes . . . that's right. Place your order, Bouncer."

"What do you mean?"

"See that microphone over there to the left? Speak into it and tell it precisely what kind of pizza you want."

"I'd like an extra-large mushroom, prune and pineapple pizza."

"EWWWWWWWWWWWW," squeaked Squeeker.

But as soon as Bouncer placed his order, mechanical hands appeared and tossed the dough, preparing a pizza in record time. Another robot popped it in the oven, and before you could say "Balloonatiks!" the pizza was done and piping hot.

"This is fabulous!" said Bouncer, taking a bite.

Flator nodded approvingly. "I could get used to this—though none of that weird food for me!"

"Now . . . I spoke to each of your parents—"

"You spoke to my father?" Bouncer asked, surprised.

"Not exactly. He put me on hold for three hours. I finally gave up and talked to your mother."

"That figures."

"Your parents think this could work. But there's another part to this deal. It's behind that door over there."

The Balloonatiks opened the door.

"A CLASSROOM!!" They all shouted in horror.

"Yes, a classroom. This is to be a boarding school. A special boarding school. Those computers you saw and those gadgets . . . they're the most sophisticated crime-fighting equipment you can imagine. And of course, all super heroes need a place to unwind. That's why I invented that pizza oven and set up the coolest hang-out in all of Hot Air City for you."

"Cool," said Sparky.

"And in each of your rooms, you'll find the things you love. Sparky . . . yours has a karaoke machine so you can practice singing. And Squeeker, yours has a canopy bed done in purple just like at home. I'm sorry it no longer color-coordinates to you, but it's the best I could do.

Flator, yours has weights and a television with a super satellite I invented so it airs nothing but sports twenty-four hours a day. Airbrain, yours has a powerful computer and a mini laboratory. And Bouncer, yours is loaded with gags."

"Chattering teeth?"

"Yes, chattering teeth and all."

"I'm lovin' it, Pop!" Flator grew in size.

"But . . ."

"Here it comes . . . the bad news," said Flator, shrinking.

"You also have to go to school here. I'll be your teacher, and I expect you all to get excellent grades and do well . . . or the gadgets go."

"Do I have to do well in math? I hate math," moaned Bouncer.

"Sure," said Sparky. "Bouncer hates math, but watch how he can count pizzas!"

"You all will do well. Now . . . I have one last thing to show you. Follow me."

Professor Swellhead led them out onto the estate grounds and over to what looked like an air-

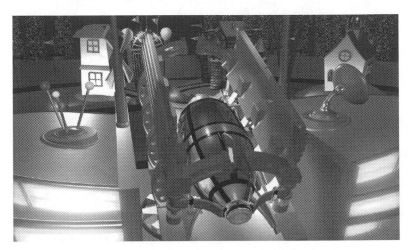

plane hangar. He pressed a button and out arose a blimp. A Balloonatik blimp with amazing colors and emblazoned with the letter "B" on the side.

"WOW!" said Airbrain.

"Yes, Airbrain. This is a WOW. Because most blimps can only move at certain speeds. This blimp can fly like a rocket. Care to go for a ride?"

The five Balloonatiks needed to hear no more. They scrambled over each other to get the best seats on the blimp.

"10 . . . 9 . . . 8 . . . oh , what the heck . . . BLAST-OFF!" shouted Professor Swellhead shouted as they shot up to the sky.

"Look!" screeched Squeeker, "there's my house!"

"A house? You call that a house? I live in a house," Sparky said, "that's a mansion. It's a hundred houses rolled into one!"

They flew into the sky, looking down on Hot Air City with its buildings, schools, parks . . . and its pollution and too many cars . . . before Professor Swellhead brought them in safely for a landing.

"Well, Balloonatiks? Are you going to remain five different kids or are you going to become a team? It's your choice."

Bouncer looked at Airbrain. "I'm sorry I sat on you before."

"It's OK, Bouncer."

"Do you have anything to say, Flator?" Professor Swellhead asked.

"Sorry I made fun of you Bouncer. But I'm still a muscleman."

"What are you going to decide?"

The five Balloonatiks looked at each other.

"WE DECIDE YES!"

CHAPTER 10

Leaky's Luck

After the Balloonatiks were settled into their new home and school, Professor Swellhead called a meeting in their huge hang-out room.

"All crime-fighters and super heroes have crimes to fight and people needing rescuing," he said. "But we have a frog to find—Leaky. A rude little frog, I may add."

"So we need to rescue the little, green slimy thing," said Bouncer, in between bites of mushroom, prune and pineapple pizza, "but just how do we do that?"

"Good question. Well, the blimp is equipped with a satellite camera, so while we were taking our ride, I programmed our computer to take photographs of Hot Air City. Maybe the pictures will provide some clues."

"Clues . . . " squeaked Squeeker, "How exciting! We're like real detectives. Gang, doesn't that make you want to stand up and cheer?"

In his most sarcastic voice, Flator just said, "Rah, rah."

Professor Swellhead moved over to the computers and TV screens, popped in a tape, and they watched Hot Air City come up on the screen. Most of the pictures the blimp took were boring.

"Man walking dog." The computer's voice analyzed the pictures, telling them what was on the screen. "Woman buying newspaper. Pizza delivery person delivering pizza. Man walking dog. Woman walking dog." The computer's voice went on and on.

"Schoolchildren playing soccer. Little girl jumping rope."

"Professor, isn't there some other way to find Leaky? This is boring. How 'bout popping in a cool video. Something with that action star, Joe Jameson," said Flator.

"Please," said Sparky, "how about a documentary on the endangered flying fish of Borneo?"

"How about a documentary on Einstein?" offered Airbrain.

"Come on!" snapped Flator, inflating himself, "Einstein? You are a nerd!"

In an instant, all the Balloonatiks were arguing about movies and videos. In fact, they were arguing so loudly, they almost didn't hear what the computer said next.

"Strange creature walking with sack."

"Stop, XTR3000. Repeat," said Professor Swellhead.

"Strange creature walking with sack."

All five Balloonatiks looked at the computer.

"WHAT?!?" They all yelled.

"Enlarge that picture, XTR3000."

There, on their huge computer screen, stood a mean-looking creature. A completely strange-looking creature. A creature that looked like he was made of rubber.

"What the heck is that, Professor Dude?" asked Flator.

"I believe that is our frog-napper," said Professor Swellhead.

"Then that is our only chance of getting back to our human selves," said Flator. "Come on, Balloonatiks! We need that frog! So let's get in the blimp and go find this goopified guy."

Professor Swellhead and the Balloonatiks raced for the blimp. Airbrain, Squeeker, Flator, Sparky and the professor climbed aboard.

"Where's Bouncer?" Airbrain asked as Professor Swellhead slid behind the control seat.

"Here he comes!" pointed Sparky.

Bouncer climbed aboard.

"What took you so long?" Sparky demanded.

"I wanted to grab a pizza. We could be out all night looking for this guy. And I also needed my backpack."

"What for?" Sparky asked him, hands on her hips.

"My gags. You never know when you're going to need a whoopee cushion or a pair of chattering teeth. PFFFFFFFFFFFFFFFFFFFFFFFFT!"

Sparky rolled her eyes. "You're pathetic! Professor Swellhead, let's fly this thing!"

Professor Swellhead pressed his blast-off button, and they were zooming through the skies over Hot Air City in no time.

"Do you realize if we get Leaky, I'll be back to the cheerleading squad in time for the big competition! I may even get to enter the Miss Hot Air City contest!" Squeeker exclaimed excitedly.

"Rah, rah," said Flator in his most sarcastic voice.

"Look! There he is!" shouted Airbrain.

The Balloonatiks and Pop looked down. The creature was enormous, and he sure looked mad!

"This is a job for Airbrain," Airbrain said with glee. He pressed his seat ejector button, which propelled him out of the blimp and toward their enemy. Airbrain flew through the sky and landed with a bounce on the giant gooped creature that was terrorizing the citizens of Hot Air City. But the creature picked up tiny Airbrain and flung him back into the blimp.

"Ouch!" Airbrain said as he landed in his seat with a thud.

"Oh, Airbrain, are you all OK? Poor baby," Squeeker said, rushing to his side.

"I'm fine now," Airbrain sighed, smiling at his secret love.

"What's with this gooped geek?" asked Flator. He was getting angry and increasing in size.

Pop landed the blimp, and Flator took off to attack the creature.

"Hey, you big goop-head. Look over here!" Flator waved his arms and started inflating, but the creature just flicked his finger and Flator ended up half-popped and lying on the ground.

"I'd say we're dealing with a DEFLATOR," joked Bouncer.

"The problem is we're not working together as a team," Squeeker said. "You can make fun of me all you want, but I know that a cheerleading squad needs to pull together. So come on team!" With that she leaped high in the air and did a cartwheel.

Sparky rolled her eyes. "I think you're right about the teamwork thing, but I am not shaking any pom-poms. Let's come up with a plan so we can get Leaky back!"

The five Balloonatiks and Professor Swellhead gathered in a huddle. Meanwhile, Deflator continued stomping through the city, holding the sack containing Leaky.

"We need a plan, Professor. That guy's a monster!" said Bouncer.

"And gigantic!" said Flator.

"And kind of mean," said Airbrain, rubbing his arm where Deflator had grabbed him.

Professor Swellhead said, "This is no time to

panic, kids. He may be big. He may be scary. But you all have to remember your powers. Each of you has something you can use to defeat him. And always, brains can beat muscle . . . we just have to think."

The gang put their heads together and formulated a plan. When they were through, Squeeker was ready to lead the way.

"Ready team?" shouted Squeeker.

"READY!" They all shouted.

"OK, then. Hubba, hubba, we're made of rubba! Now let's go get that goopster!" Squeeker cheered.

The five Balloonatiks raced towards Deflator, each ready to do his or her part of their plan.

Bouncer took a deep breath and transformed himself into a giant bowling ball, crashing into Deflator and upsetting his balance.

"Flator, go!" Bouncer shouted.

Flator let himself get mad—really mad. He increased his size to enormous proportions and sat on Deflator, pinning him to the ground.

"Hand off to Airbrain," Flator yelled out.

Airbrain hovered over Deflator and sucked in all the air he could. Then he blew a hurricane force wind to keep Deflator struggling in the blustery weather.

"Go Squeeker! Your turn now!"

"SCREEEEEEEEEEEEEEEEEEEEEEEEEEEEECH !!!!!!!!!!!!!!!!"

Squeeker squeeked so loudly that Deflator had to cover his ears, releasing the sack containing Leaky, which Airbrain then scooped up.

"Way to go!"

And for good measure, Sparky zapped Deflator with a few lightening bolts.

"That'll teach you, goop-brain!"

Deflator fought back, screaming "I'll get you, you rotten Balloonatiks!" Deflator started grabbing at them, finally catching Sparky in his grasp.

"Someone help me, I'm all sparked out!"

"That does it!" shouted Bouncer. He raced to his backpack and pulled out four sets of chattering teeth. He hurled them with all his might at

Deflator. The teeth grabbed hold of Deflator and bit down. Chatter, chatter, chatter. CHOMP! CHOMP! CHOMP! Finally, one last chomp sprung a leak in Deflator and freed Sparky. Deflator flew into the sky with a HISSSSSSSSSSSSSSSSSSSSS and the Balloonatiks had Leaky!

"We did it! We did it!" cheered Squeeker.

While the Balloonatiks were excitedly rushing over to Pop, happy with their accomplishment, Deflator was flying backwards through the sky roaring, "You haven't seen the last of me. Revenge will be sweet!"

"I'm sure we haven't seen the last of him. And what worries me is he must have gotten hold of some of the goop," muttered Pop. Then, brightening, he turned to the Balloonatiks. "We won't worry about Deflator right now. You did a good job, kids. I'm very proud of you, and I'm sure Leaky here is proud of you, too."

"Hubba, hubba, Balloonatiks!" Squeeker turned a cartwheel.

Pop opened the sack and out hopped Leaky.

Leaky looked up at the five Balloonatiks and loudly burped.

"That's gratitude for you," Flator said.

"Come on," said Sparky. "Let's go home."

Later, hanging out in the hideaway, the Balloonatiks rested. They had eaten a total of seven pizzas and four enormous ice cream sundaes. Everyone was stuffed and sleepy.

"Come on, gang," Squeeker squeaked. "We did it. No pooping out! We popped Deflator! We really can be super heroes. In fact, I have a cheer."

Bouncer moaned, "Not another cartwheel. Please, Squeeker." He made his whoopee cushion sound. "PFFFFFFFFFTTTTTTTTTTTTTTTTTTTT!"

"You're gross," said Squeeker. "But I put you in my cheer anyway."

> Bouncer, Bouncer, he's our man, if he can't pop him, nobody can.

> Airbrain, Airbrain, he's our guy, if you need help, he knows how to fly.

> Flator, Flator, he's the dude, he can grow fifty feet tall when he's in the mood.

Sparky, Sparky, she's a real live wire,
and if you don't like it, that girl's on fire.

Squeeker, Squeeker, she's right here, but
her voice will make you cover your ears.

Then Squeeker turned three cartwheels.

"That was TERRIBLE!" moaned Bouncer.

"I thought she was wonderful," sighed Airbrain.

Leaky just burped.

"I'm not finished!" Squeeker exclaimed.

"Hubba, hubba, we're made out of rubba! Goooooooooooo Balloonatiks!!"

The other four just stared.

"Come on," Squeeker squeaked, "are we a team or not?"

Flator just said, "Rah, rah."

"Flator!" she squeaked back.

"OK, OK, we're a team."

"What did you say?"

Flator grinned.

"I said 'Rah, rah!'" and with that all five Balloonatiks began cheering and laughing.

And Leaky just smiled. And burped.

About the Author and Creator of the Balloonatiks Books

The Balloonatiks were created from the imagination of Tony Diloia, founder of Animagic Entertainment. Animagic is a ten-year-old cartoon character development company with offices in New York City and Santa Barbara. In his free time, Tony enjoys the beach near his home in California with his family.

Based on Tony's characters, these books are written by Erica Orloff. Erica is a published author and book editor. She regularly speaks to schoolchildren about publishing and writing. Erica lives in Florida with her family and their menagerie of dogs, rabbits, parrots and other assorted birds.

BALLOONATIKS FAN CLUB

Can you say *"Hubba hubba, we're made of rubba"* ten times fast? If you can, write to us at:

Animagic Entertainment
P.O. Box 880581
Boca Raton, FL
33488-0581

Include your name and address and we'll send you something fun, and automatically sign you up for our fan club so we can mail you information about upcoming television episodes, behind-the-scenes stories, new books, and cool products.

Hubba, Hubba

Alexa Milo

President

Isabella Diaz

Vice President

Nicholas Diaz

Treasurer

Coming Soon from the Balloonatiks

VOLUME 2
Balloonatiks:
Deflator's Revenge

Meet the Balloonatik's arch enemy: Deflator. Jealous of the kids' mentor, Professor "Pop" Swellhead, Deflator plans to "goop" all of Hot Air City—starting with the graduating class of Hot Air High. It's a race against time to stop him . . . Can they do it?

VOLUME 3
Balloonatiks:
The Great Computer Caper

The Millennium Bug has struck Hot Air City . . . and now the Balloonatiks are stuck inside a computer in a virtual reality world. Only Airbrain, with his computer skills, can devise a program to save them. Race with the Balloonatiks from dot.com site to dot.com site as they try to escape cyberspace.

VOLUME 4
Balloonatiks:
ZZZZAPPED!!!

The Zapper is loose and turning Hot Air City into an electric disaster. Only Sparky, doubting her role as a Balloonatik, can save the city from short-circuiting. But can she believe in herself enough to challenge him in the skies over town? As the sky lights up in an electrical display of wizardry, she'll learn the answer, along with her friends!